Pocket Protest

*Also by Anna Branford*

Violet Mackerel's Brilliant Plot

Violet Mackerel's Remarkable Recovery

Violet Mackerel's Natural Habitat

Violet Mackerel's Personal Space

Violet Mackerel's Possible Friend

# Pocket Protest

Anna Branford

illustrated by
Elanna Allen

atheneum
Atheneum Books for Young Readers
New York London Toronto Sydney New Delhi

*Atheneum Books for Young Readers*
An imprint of Simon & Schuster Children's Publishing Division
1230 Avenue of the Americas, New York, New York 10020

Also available in an Atheneum Books for Young Readers hardcover edition
Book design by Lauren Rille
The text for this book is set in Excelsior.
The illustrations for this book are rendered in pencil with digital ink.
Manufactured in the United States of America
0814 FFG
First US Edition
10 9 8 7 6 5 4 3 2 1
Library of Congress Cataloging-in-Publication Data
Branford, Anna.
Violet Mackerel's pocket protest / Anna Branford ; illustrated by Elanna Allen. — 1st US edition.
p. cm.
"Originally published in 2013 by Walker Books Australia Pty Ltd"—Copyright page.
Summary: Violet and Rose organize a protest to save the big oak tree in Clover Park.
ISBN 978-1-4424-9458-9 (hardcover)
ISBN 978-1-4424-9459-6 (paperback)
ISBN 978-1-4424-9460-2 (eBook)
[1. Protest movements—Fiction. 2. Oak—Fiction. 3. Trees—Fiction.
4. Environmental protection—Fiction.] I. Allen, Elanna, illustrator. II. Title.
PZ7.B737384Vho 2014
[Fic]—dc23 2013035382

For Lisa (my friend)

—A. B.

For Anna

—E. A.

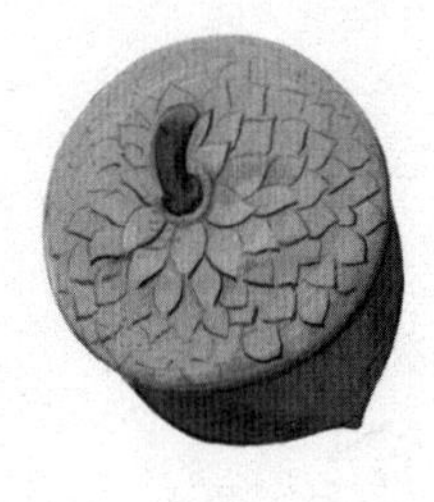

Pocket Protest

# 1 The Oak Tree

Violet Mackerel is under the big, old oak tree at Clover Park. She is collecting acorns with Rose, her very good friend and neighbor. So far they have about twenty each, but they are still looking for more, mainly because it is nice to be under

the oak tree where the sun filters through yellowish-green, the smells are musty and earthy, and small creatures sometimes rustle and scurry in the leaves.

Just as their pockets are getting too full to hold many more acorns, a truck pulls up and two people get out. They are dressed in matching green overalls with red writing that says JOHNSON'S TREE SERVICES.

Violet wonders what sort of work they might do. Rose guesses

that tree servicers might be a bit like waiters at a restaurant, except instead of bringing drinks in tall glasses on trays, they bring them in buckets and hoses. Violet suspects they could be a bit like doctors, only instead of counting heartbeats and listening to deep breaths, they count acorns and listen to rustling leaves. They both think that when they are older they might like to have matching overalls that say VIOLET AND ROSE'S TREE SERVICES.

The people in the van walk over to the tree, so Rose is able to ask them what they do instead of guessing. They say that their work isn't much like being a waiter or a doctor, but they don't really have time to explain what it *is* like. Mainly they just need Violet and Rose to move away so they can measure different parts of

the tree and take pictures without being disturbed.

Vincent is sitting nearby on a wooden bench reading a book called *Honeymooning on a Shoestring*. He and Violet's mama got married quite a while ago now, but there wasn't enough money for a honeymoon, so they are thinking of having a late one. Violet has had lots of good ideas for them, like scuba diving in the ocean or possibly going to space. But there is still not much money for a honeymoon, especially not one that involves diving equipment or rockets, so they definitely need the shoestring sort. That is why Vincent and Violet borrowed the book from the library.

Violet and Rose both feel a bit shy after being asked to move away from the oak tree, so they join Vincent on the bench and look at the book with him. The bench is their second favorite place in the park because it has a nice goldish plaque that says IN MEMORY OF EVA.

It twinkles as if the dusty old wood is wearing a brooch. They like wondering who Eva might have been.

"What do you think those people are doing?" Violet asks Vincent.

But before he can answer, the woman in the overalls calls out and asks if there is a gas station nearby. Vincent is a bit deaf, so he has to go up quite close to hear her question properly and ends up talking with them for a little while.

"Did they tell you anything?"

asks Rose when he joins them back on the bench with a slight frown on his face.

"Yes," says Vincent. "They told me they've been hired to cut down the oak tree."

"Cut it *down*?" checks Violet.

"Cut it *right* down?" double-checks Rose.

Vincent nods. "There is going to be a parking lot built over this part of the park, and they need to clear the land before laying down the concrete."

"They can't do that!" says Violet.

"Unfortunately, they can," says Vincent. "They're coming back in two weeks to do the job."

It is a horrible surprise.

Before leaving, the people from Johnson's Tree Services bang a big sign onto the tree with a noisy hammer. It says:

It is quite late in the day now, so the birds are getting a bit noisy. The cicadas have started singing, and the insects are turning golden in the setting sunlight. Violet, Vincent, and Rose do the slow, quiet walking that people do after they find out something worrying.

When they get to Violet's house, Violet and Rose go up to Violet's room to talk and think. They have told each other their best secrets under the oak tree. They have found

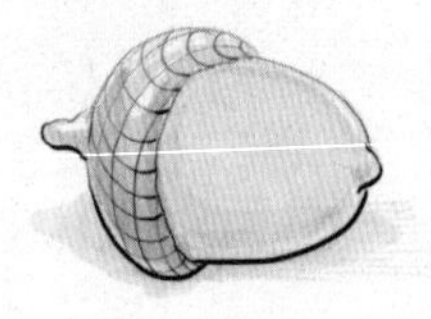

some very good small things there too—not just acorns, but leaf skeletons and a butterfly wing and even a golden dollar coin. Once they made a daisy chain that went all the

way around the trunk. It is hard to

imagine the park without the oak tree.

"Do you have any theories that might help?" asks Rose. Violet has theories about lots of things, and they are sometimes useful for solving problems.

Violet thinks. "No," she says. "Maybe it's because my theories are mostly about small things, and this is a very, very big thing."

Rose thinks too. "Johnson's Tree Services said the chopping won't actually happen for two weeks," she says. "There must be *something* we can do before then."

Violet agrees, but she doesn't know what that something could be. That is the problem.

## 2 The Enormous Protest

At dinnertime it is just Violet, Vincent, and Violet's big sister, Nicola, because Rose has gone home and Mama and Violet's big brother, Dylan, are at a violin recital. They talk about the problem of the oak tree. Vincent says he is going to write a letter to the local newspaper, which Violet thinks is a very good idea. But she is still hoping for a good idea of her own.

"You could try holding a protest," Nicola says. "Lara and I organized one at school last year."

Violet remembers Nicola and Lara's protest. The sports department had planned to turn one of the art studios into a sports equipment room because there wasn't enough space for all the hoops and bats and they said hardly anyone was using the studio. But Nicola and her best friend, Lara, did use it, almost every day. So they started a petition, which they told Violet is a long list of names and signatures of people who think something is important. Their friends and even some of their teachers signed it. Nicola and Lara dressed up as artists in berets and artists' smocks and carried big card-board signs that said SAVE OUR STU-DIO and RIGHTS FOR ARTISTS NOW. They marched around the school doing a chant they made up, which Violet remembers because they practiced it quite a lot in Nicola's room.

*One, two, three, four.*

*We won't take it anymore.*

*Five, six, seven, eight.*

*We need spaces to create.*

*Eight, seven, six, five.*

*Keep art in*

*our school alive.*

*Four, three, two, one.*

*Or its beauty*

*will be gone.*

It was a very good chant, Violet thought.

After dinner, Violet, Vincent, and Nicola watch a television show about vacations. Vincent is hoping there might be a shoestring segment, but the show is more the sort with hotels and pools and spas and towels cleverly folded into the shape of a bird. Violet wishes there could be folded-bird towels on Mama and Vincent's honeymoon. But mainly she is too busy thinking about other things.

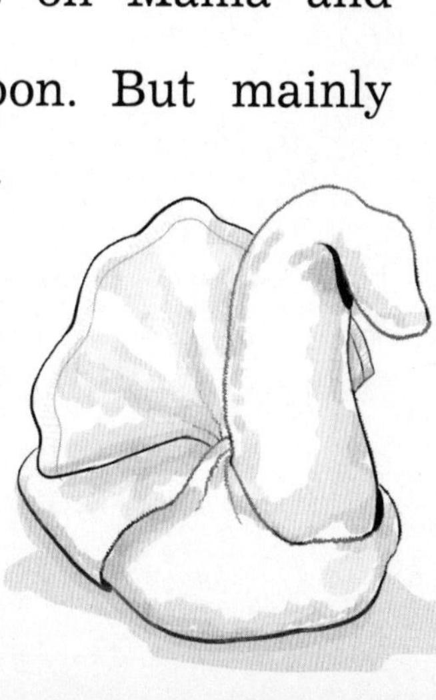

Violet's mind's eye is seeing herself and Rose leading an enormous protest, wearing very good costumes. Violet has a tree costume with eyeholes and leafy branches, and Rose has a bird costume with a built-in

nest and eggs. They are marching around the park, holding a big sign that says SAVE OUR OAK TREE. Their petition is as long as a dictionary. A huge crowd of people is following them, and some of the people are dressed up too, as trees, birds, and other animals whose natural habitat is the oak tree. (Although, their costumes are not quite as nice as Violet's and Rose's.) They are doing a special tree-saving chant, which Violet's mind's ear can't quite hear yet. But her mind's eye is doing a very good job of seeing a little plane writing SAY NO TO CHOPPING across the sky above the park. It would be an excellent protest, Violet thinks.

It is just about bedtime, so Violet

says thank you to Nicola for the good idea and goes up to her room to put on her pajamas and think a bit more. She wishes it was not too late to go over to Rose's house and tell her about the enormous protest and the little plane. It would also be good to see if Rose has any ideas to solve some of the problems Violet is already starting to think of too.

For example, at Nicola's school there were quite a lot of people there to see the costumes and read the signs and hear the chanting and join the protest. But except for Violet and Rose and Vincent, there is usually no one in the park at all apart from some small animals that are not very good at protesting. So who would see? Also, big signs and costumes and a small plane are quite a lot to organize, especially in only two weeks.

When Mama gets back from the violin recital, she comes upstairs to say good night, and Violet tells her about the oak tree and the parking lot and Johnson's Tree Services.

"Do you think there is even a small chance we will be able to save the oak tree?" Violet asks.

"If the decision has already been made, then probably only a very small chance," says Mama. "But that doesn't mean it's not worth

trying, if it's for something very important."

Mama has some vacation brochures in her hand, and Violet suspects she is thinking of the important honeymoon as well as the important oak tree. But as she goes to sleep, she thinks about what Mama has said. The oak tree *is* very important. So it *is* worth trying.

The next morning is Saturday, which is market day for the Mackerels and Vincent. They have a stall with Mama's knitted things on one side and Vincent's china birds on the other and a section in the middle where china birds sit in small knitted nests. Violet likes the middle section best, and when she goes with them to the market, it is her job to choose the right nest for the right bird. But this morning Violet is going to Rose's house instead. She is going to take her notebook in case they need to do some plotting.

Even though it is normal for the Mackerels and Vincent to wake up very early on Saturday mornings, lots of other people sleep in on that day, so Mama says Violet needs to wait for quite a while before she goes next door. Violet uses the extra time to work on a chant about saving the oak tree.

She would quite like to write one with numbers like Nicola and Lara's, so she starts by writing *One, two, three, four* in her notebook. Unfortunately, there are not very many oak-tree-related words that rhyme with "four." However, Violet has been doing fractions at school, and she has the good idea of trying those. She writes *One, two, two-and-a-half, three*, which turns out to rhyme quite well with *Please do not chop*

*down our tree*. Violet smiles. Then she draws possible costumes for herself and Rose until it is time to go next door.

Rose and her mama are having breakfast smoothies from their special smoothie maker when Violet arrives, and there is enough left over for Violet to have one too. Rose is quite excited to hear about the petition and the signs and the little plane. She also likes the chant and the tree and bird costumes.

She agrees, though, about the problem of there being no people in the park to join the protest and also about the slight trickiness of organizing even a very small plane. But Rose's mama says there is some cardboard in the recycling so at least they can start by making a sign.

They find two cereal boxes that they open up and stick together with sticky tape to make one biggish piece of cardboard. On the gray side where there aren't any pictures of

cereal, Rose writes *save our oak tree* because her writing is the neatest, and Violet draws the tree because her tree drawings are quite good. They have to leave a little space where the tape is because the pens don't draw there. Violet and Rose look carefully at their work. It is not a *bad* sign. But it is not much like the one in their minds' eyes.

Rose frowns. "I think for an *enormous* protest, what we need is a really *big* sign," she says, "so everyone will see it and want to join us. I'm not sure if anyone will notice a small grayish sign."

Violet thinks. "Rose," she says, "you and I would notice a small sign, no matter what color it was."

"We would *especially* notice a sign if it was small," agrees Rose.

"And we are the sort of people who mind a lot about things like tree chopping."

Rose nods, and Violet thinks a bit more.

"It *might* be that the sort of people who notice small signs are the sort who care most about small things," Violet says. "Things like birds not having nests and people not having a place to collect acorns."

Rose smiles. Violet writes her idea down in her notebook. She calls it the Theory of Seeing Small Things.

"That is a very good theory," says Rose.

Although the cereal boxes were the biggest pieces of cardboard in

Rose's recycling, there are lots of smaller pieces that are not gray and do not have pictures on them. They are perfect for making small signs that say catchy things like:

and there is still space underneath to write SAVE OUR OAK TREE, so people will know exactly what they mean. Violet and Rose make quite a lot of small signs while they practice the fractions chant.

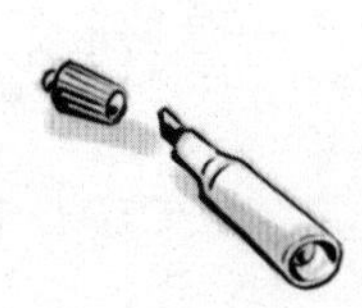

Late that afternoon, when Mama and Vincent are back from the market, Vincent would like to finish reading *Honeymooning on a Shoestring*, so he goes with Violet and Rose to Clover Park again. Their small signs are just the right size to carry in their pockets.

They put a few of them in special places along the path that runs through the park, and Vincent helps with the high-up places. Violet and Rose also do their chant, even though no one is there to hear it except for Vincent. They also do a sort of protesting dance, which ends up going around the trunk of the oak tree.

"Don't worry, ants," says Violet to three small black ones crawling up the trunk. "We're going to save your home."

"Don't worry, birds," calls

Rose up into the branches. "We're going to save your nests."

If Violet and Rose stand on opposite sides of the tree and give it a very big hug, they find that they can hold hands around it.

"Don't worry, oak tree," whispers Violet into the scratchy bark.

"We are doing our very best to help," whispers Rose.

They stay under the oak tree for a long time.

Violet saves the last of the small signs to tweak between the wooden slats under the Eva brooch on the bench. After that, Violet and Rose look around at the protest they have begun. It is quite different from the enormous one their minds' eyes first saw. This is more of a pocket protest. But they quite like it and are both feeling very hopeful about the Theory of Seeing Small Things. Perhaps someone who cares about small things will spot one of the signs and know exactly what to do to save the oak tree. Even though the wind is picking up and the leaves

are starting to rustle together, hardly any of the signs are blowing away.

Vincent is feeling quite hopeful too. He and Mama sold a lot of china birds and knitted things at the market this morning, so they really might be able to do one or two of the ideas in his honeymoon book.

But when Violet and Vincent arrive back home after saying good-bye to Rose, some bad news is waiting for them, which is rather a lot of water on the floor.

Mama and Nicola are mopping it up with towels, and Dylan is building a dam of socks in the laundry doorway to stop the water from flowing out. Everyone is in a slight panic.

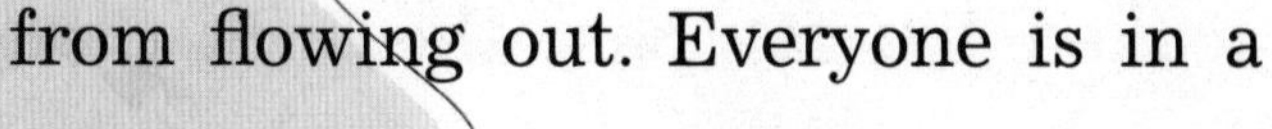

"The washing machine leaked," says Mama, handing some dripping towels to Vincent to wring out over the sink.

Violet adds more socks to Dylan's sock dam and watches the water puddling in the laundry.

Even though it seems like quite a big flood at first, the water has not leaked too far past the sock dam, and with all five of them working, it doesn't take very long to clean it up. Violet doesn't mind the feeling of bare feet on wet towels, with warmish soapy water coming up between her toes. Plus, the laundry floor looks quite a lot cleaner than it did before. But Mama and Vincent look a bit gloomy.

Later on, when Violet is having some warm milk before bed, Vincent says it will be hard to get by in a house with five people and no washing machine. By the end of one week, that is seventy socks alone (which is why Dylan and Violet were able to build such a good dam). And the Mackerels and Vincent wear a lot of other clothes besides socks. Mama says the washing machine was already quite old and is beyond repair, and they will have to use the honeymoon savings to buy a new one.

"Oh well." Mama sighs. "It was fun thinking about the honeymoon anyway." Vincent gives her a hug and so does Violet.

Even though Violet had been

feeling hopeful on the walk home from the park, she is feeling a lot less hopeful now. Mama has put the vacation brochures and her list of favorite honeymoon ideas away in a drawer, and she is sighing and unpicking part of her knitting that has gone a bit wrong. Vincent is calling his friend Buzz to see if he can help with the washing machine in the morning.

Violet is sad that Mama and Vincent will not be having a honeymoon, not even the shoestring sort. And there is another reason Violet is feeling glum. The small wind that was rustling the leaves at the park has grown into quite a strong one, and now the sound of rain is starting to batter against the window. Normally that is a sound Violet especially likes. But not when she is thinking of the small signs blowing and washing away.

Violet makes one last small sign on a piece of paper from her notebook, just to cheer herself up. She writes *rights for honeymooners*. In the corner she draws a towel that has been cleverly folded into the shape of a bird. Before she goes to bed, she sticks the sign on the fridge with a magnet.

The Theory of Seeing Small Things might be trickier than it first seemed. Not even Violet or Rose would notice a small sign in the park that had been washed or blown away. And the only people who will see the honeymoon sign on the fridge are her family, and they all wanted Mama and Vincent to have a honeymoon anyway.

The next morning it is still drizzling, but there is a nice cheering smell coming from the kitchen because Sunday is the day that Vincent makes pancakes. Today he is making quite a few extra because his friend Buzz is coming and Buzz never says no to a pancake. Neither does Rose, who arrives under a beautiful umbrella

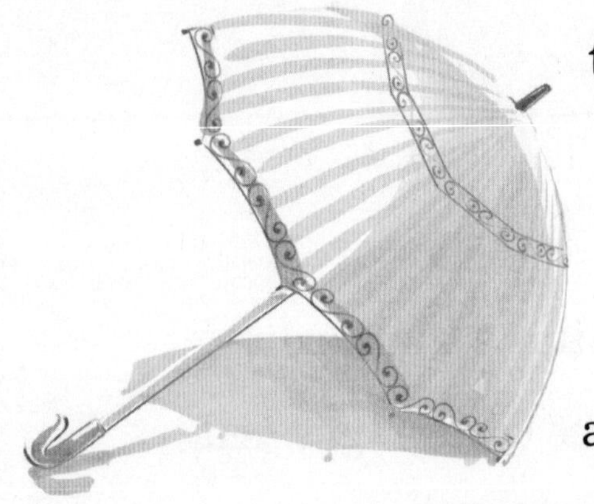

that her papa brought back from Japan. It looks a bit like an upside-down teacup without a handle.

After breakfast, Violet and Rose help with washing up while Vincent and Buzz carry the old, broken washing machine out to Buzz's truck.

"I think our small signs probably floated away in the rain last night," Rose says to Violet as soon as they are alone in Violet's room.

"Maybe the Theory of Seeing Small Things is not such a good theory after all," says Violet.

Rose thinks. "Or maybe it is a *very* good theory," she suggests, "but we just need to try it another way."

It is nice, when you are not feeling very hopeful, if someone else is feeling hopeful enough for two.

"The problem," says Rose, "is that small signs are not waterproof. I wish we had lots of mini umbrellas."

Violet looks at Rose's beautiful Japanese umbrella. "I think I might be having an idea," she says.

Violet still has the whole pocketful of acorns from the oak tree minus one acorn cap that she put on a small doll's head as a hat.

Violet quite likes the way acorn caps look like hats. But now she realizes that they look slightly like umbrellas, too.

Violet gets out her notebook. Using very tiny writing, Violet writes in one straight line: *Save the Clover Park oak tree!*

She cuts the line out very carefully with her scissors and rolls it round her little finger. Then she takes an acorn out of its cap and puts the small message inside instead. It uncurls just enough to fit perfectly around the inside of the cap.

Rose smiles and turns it upside down. It is the perfect hiding spot for a small message and it is also a perfect umbrella.

Rose writes *The Clover Park oak tree needs your help!* in the notebook. Then she cuts it out, curls it, and puts it in another of the caps.

It takes quite a long time, but Violet and Rose do not stop until all the acorn caps have small messages curled inside them. Then Rose runs home and brings back the pocketful that she collected from the oak tree, and they put messages in those, too. It is a big job, but they don't mind at all.

In the afternoon Rose has her swimming lesson, so she is going to leave an acorn message in the changing room at the pool and another at the machine where you can buy chips.

After Rose has gone home to change into her swimsuit, Violet goes with Mama to take a basket of knitted autumn leaves to Mama's friend's shop that sells knitted things. Violet tucks an acorn message in among the woolly leaves. Then she puts another on the head of a small doll in the shop. Most people will probably mistake it for an ordinary doll hat. But another sort of person might notice it there and pick it up and look inside.

When Violet and Mama get home, Vincent and Buzz have finished installing the new washing machine. Violet helps Vincent put a big load of washing in right away, and there is a nice soft humming sound instead of the clanging and banging of the old one. Violet didn't mind the clanging and banging. She minds the problem of Mama and Vincent's honeymoon much more. But she quite likes listening to the humming while she thinks about the sorts of people who might be uncurling small acorn messages.

Later on when Vincent goes to the mailbox to mail the letter about the oak tree to the local newspaper, Violet goes with him so she can leave an acorn message on the step of a little chapel they pass and another beside the mailbox.

# 6 The Short Petition

The next few days are school days, so there is not much time to go to the park as there is homework in the evenings and everyone is busy. Violet and Rose both keep acorn messages in their pockets so they can leave one whenever they see a good spot. They go to different schools, so it is quite interesting to hear about each other's hiding spots. On the afternoons when they don't see each other because Rose is horse riding or at the dentist, or Violet has gone with Mama to her knitting group, they leave notes in a special hole they once discovered in the fence between their two back gardens. The notes say things like:

Dear Violet,

Today I left an acorn message in the ball box at the tennis court and another in the shampoo aisle at the supermarket. Did you find any good places?

Love from Rose

And

Dear Rose,
Yes, today I put an acorn message by the drinking fountain and another in the pocket of a cardigan at the secondhand shop.
Love from Violet

On Friday afternoon, when no one has anything important they need to do and Vincent doesn't mind going to Clover Park, Violet and Rose are quite excited to see if anything interesting has happened. Perhaps a few people will have read their acorn messages by now and who knows what sorts of things they might have done to help. Most of all, they are hoping that the big **TREE REMOVAL** sign will have been taken down and perhaps a small sign will have been left in its place that says **PUBLIC NOTICE—TREE TO STAY**.

But actually, when they arrive at the oak tree, everything is exactly as it was before. The notice is still up, and it still says **TREE REMOVAL**.

There are no protesters gathering or news reporters saying into their microphones, "Plans to remove the oak tree have been abandoned due to a very successful pocket protest including small signs and acorn messages. This is Isabel Albatross reporting from Clover Park." It is all a bit disappointing.

Violet and Rose look around to see if they can spot any of their small signs from last weekend. They only find two, which have been blown into the bushes and are much too crumpled and rained on to be read. Even the one Violet tweaked between the wooden slats of the bench with the brooch is gone. That is the most discouraging thing of all.

Violet and Rose lie quietly under the oak tree and look up into the leafy branches and think together.

Suddenly, Rose says, "What about the petition?"

It sounds a bit like a sneeze, so

Violet says, “Bless you,” and they both giggle, which makes them feel a bit better.

"Maybe if there was a long list of people who agree with us, it would help," says Rose.

So Violet takes out her notebook, thinks very hard to remember Nicola and Lara's petition, takes her pencil out of her pocket, and writes:

We, the undersigned, do not think the oak tree should be chopped down. Lots of small animals and insects live in it. Plus it is a good place to sit under and collect acorns.

Yours sincerely,

Underneath it she signs her name and draws a small violet beside it. Rose signs her name and draws a small rose. They ask Vincent if he would like to sign the petition too, and he says he would. But that is only three names, which is not a very long petition.

Rose thinks. "One evening my mama and I were driving home past the park, and we saw a bat in the tree. I bet it would want to save the tree."

Since bats can't write, Rose writes *Bat* underneath Vincent's signature in the sort of swooping writing that bats would probably have if they could write. Then Violet has the idea of writing "bees," which she has sometimes seen buzzing in the low branches. She writes it in buzzing letters. They also add some sparrows, some ants, two grass-hoppers, a butterfly, a grayish moth with a wing injury, a black cat (who once got stuck and had to be rescued by the fire department), and a friendly huntsman spider. Then, after the small animals' and insects' signatures, they write *probably* in parentheses because Vincent says you can't actually add extra names to petitions, although he is sure that the animals would sign if they could.

Even with the added names, it is still a short petition, but it is much better than nothing. Rose slides the top of the page under the notice on the tree so that it dangles down underneath, which will hold it there for a little while at least. Perhaps no one will notice it. Perhaps more rain will come and wash it away. But for the moment, it is the only other idea Rose and Violet have for their protest.

PUBLIC
NOTICE
TREE REMOVAL
We, the undersigned, do not think the oak tree should be chopped down. Lots of small animals and insects live in it. Plus it is a good place to sit under and collect acorns.
Yours sincerely,
Violet
Rose
Butterfly
Vincent
Bat
moth
Bees
cat
Sparrow
sparrow
Spider
ant
ant
ant
grasshopper
grasshopper
(probably)

It is an early morning start for everyone in the Mackerel house the next day. Mama has three big baskets of knitted things, and Vincent has a new batch of china birds that he has been cleaning and getting ready. Nicola, who sells her handmade jewelry at the markets, has quite a lot of earrings ready too because she is saving up to buy an easel for her room. Dylan will be busking on his violin as usual. And Violet, who has been too busy with small signs and acorn messages to have anything of her own to bring to the markets, will be helping everyone as well as eating poffertjes from a cup with a stick.

Usually everyone just sits sleepily at the table at breakfast before going to the market, slightly wishing they were still in bed. But this morning when the alarm clock buzzes, even though it is not completely light yet, Vincent goes outside into the garden in his slippers to see if the newspaper has been delivered, since it sometimes comes quite early. Violet goes out in her slippers too. They are hoping the newspaper might have published his letter about the oak tree.

Vincent unrolls the paper and goes straight to the letters section. Violet looks over his shoulder. It would be quite exciting to see his name there. They look closely at the

page and check and double-check to make sure, but it is definitely not there.

"Perhaps it will be published next week," suggests Mama at breakfast.

"That will be too late," says Vincent.

"The oak tree will be gone by then," says Violet.

Violet helps load the boxes, baskets, tables, and big umbrella into the van, and they drive to the market.

It is quite a nice morning when the sun comes out, and Violet does a very good job of matching china birds with the knitted nests.

Lots of people are stopping at the stall to look at them and to try on Mama's scarves and to look closely at Nicola's earrings, and quite a few of them are buying something. Dylan is playing the new concerto he had learned for the recital, and there is a nice sound of coins dropping into his violin case now and then.

It should be a very good market day. But the pocket protest is not working, and that is all Violet can think about even as she is eating her poffertjes. Vincent is not smiling very much either. Violet suspects he is thinking about the oak tree too.

When they all arrive home from the market in the afternoon, there is a surprise on the doorstep, which is

Rose wearing a very beautiful spotty dress. Violet is not surprised about the dress because she knows Rose has been at a birthday party. But she is surprised to see her waiting on the doorstep. Rose is flapping a piece of paper in her hand.

"Look! Look!" squeals Rose as Violet clambers out from the van.

It is the short petition they left on the oak tree. Violet looks and sees right away why Rose is so excited. There are two new names on the petition, printed in very neat, curly old-fashioned writing.

*Albert Trivelli*

and

*Iva Trivelli (Probably)*

"We drove past the park on our way home from the party," says Rose, "so I asked Mama if I could hop out and check the petition, and then I saw it!"

Later in the afternoon, Mama, Nicola, and Dylan add their names to the petition, so it is a little bit longer. And after that, Violet, Rose, and Vincent go back to the park and put the slightly longer petition back underneath the **TREE REMOVAL** sign.

It is quite hard to know what to think. On the one hand, there is less than a week to go until the oak tree will be chopped, the newspaper did not publish Vincent's letter, and no one seems to have noticed the pocket protest. None of these are very cheering thoughts. But on the other hand, Albert Trivelli and Eva Trivelli (probably) have seen the short petition, and perhaps they are the sorts of people who will mind about the tree and find a good way to help.

*That* is an extremely cheering thought.

As well as sitting under the oak tree, watching the insects go golden for a little while in case it is the last weekend they can, Violet and Rose look very closely at the goldish plaque that says IN MEMORY OF EVA.

# 8 The Sunday Special

Even on Sundays there is not much sleeping in for anyone at Violet's house, and usually the waking up of people is done by Violet, who would like someone to help her open the marmalade or explain what a piccolo is. But this morning it is Vincent who wakes Violet up by sitting down on her bed with a slight bounce and a newspaper rustling noisily in his hand.

"Look! Look!" Vincent is saying. Violet opens her eyes just a crack.

"Did they publish your letter?" she asks sleepily.

"Better than that!" says Vincent.

Violet rubs her eyes and sits up so she can look properly. Then, when she sees the paper, she wonders if she is actually still asleep and dreaming. There is a huge picture of the oak tree. And beside the picture there is not just Vincent's letter. There are lots of letters. So many that instead of publishing

them with the ordinary letters on Saturday, they have all been saved up for a Sunday Special. And there is a whole section about the mystery acorn messages.

"I had no idea there were plans to cut down the beautiful old tree that my sisters and I played in as children," wrote one lady who found an acorn message at the library.

"The oak tree is the nicest part of the view from my office. It would be a terrible shame to lose it. I would like to join these protestors in their efforts to save it," wrote a man who found an acorn message at his bus stop.

Vincent and Violet are so busy

reading the letters out loud to each other and gasping and making sure that they both are really, truly awake that it takes them quite a while to notice what is on the opposite page.

It is another photo, but with tattered edges. At first Violet thinks it must be of a different oak tree because the oak tree is a bit smaller, plus there are houses with gardens behind it instead of the block of flats that are behind Clover Park. Underneath the tree there are a man and a woman with old-fashioned clothes and hats and very big smiles.

Across the bottom of the photo, someone has written *Albert and Eva Trivelli, 1948*, in faded curly writing.

"'Eighty-six-year-old Albert Trivelli was twenty-one when he and his wife, Eva, bought their first home,'" reads Vincent. "'They were married at Clover Chapel and lived in a small house with a garden looking out onto the park. Some years later, not too far away, they opened Chateau Trivelli, a small hotel still run by their son, Henry.'"

Then Violet reads out loud one of the parts where Albert is being interviewed.

"'After my wife died, I moved into a smaller home only a short walk away, and soon after that, our old house was knocked down to make room for some flats. But I still walk to the park most evenings to watch the colors in the oak tree change as the sun goes down, because that was something Eva and I always did together. That is why I built the bench there in memory of her.

"'I was terribly sad to see that the tree was to be removed and to think that no one would mind but me. But then I found a small sign on the bench near Eva's name, and I realized that at least one other person minded. Then, when I found a short petition, I realized that a few did. Even if the oak tree is removed, it will be a great comfort to me to know that other people think it is as beautiful and as special as I do.'"

At the end of the article, Vincent reads, "'In light of the concerns of local residents, the *Clover Times* has been in contact with the council to discuss the preservation of the oak tree at Clover Park.'"

Violet and Vincent do a noisy sort of dance together, and it goes all the way to Vincent and Mama's room, where Mama is still trying to be slightly asleep. But she wakes up quite quickly, and she doesn't mind

Violet and Vincent excitedly reading the letters and the article out loud to her, even if sometimes they are reading different parts at the same time.

Violet, Rose, and Vincent decide they will go to the park a bit later than normal to see if Albert Trivelli comes to watch the colors changing in the oak tree as the sun goes down. They would all like to meet him. Vincent says if they arrive at about the time they normally leave, which is when the birds and cicadas are at their noisiest and the insects are almost perfectly gold, they might be able to find him there. Violet and Rose think it is an excellent idea.

There is no one at the park when they arrive, but they decide to sit and wait for a while, just in case.

When the green leaves start to turn slightly purple in the changing light, a man appears on the path. He is much, much older than the man in the photo in the newspaper, and he walks with a stick. He is wearing a hat, and Violet and Rose feel almost certain that it is Albert Trivelli. But it isn't until they smile and wave and he smiles and waves back that they are sure. Because he walks quite slowly and it is too exciting to wait for him to reach the bench, they run over to say hello.

"Was it you who made the

small signs and the petition?" Albert asks Violet and Rose.

"Yes!" they answer together.

Albert shows them the sign they had tweaked between the slats of the bench. It has been folded in his pocket.

"It cheers me up every time I look at it," he tells them.

It is a bit of a squish to fit all four of them on Eva's bench, but they do eventually manage it. Albert shows them how, after turning gold and then purple, the leaves go almost navy blue before they turn into black shadows against the darkening sky.

"Will you come back to our place and have a cup of tea with us?" asks Vincent when there are no more colors to see.

"Well, why not," says Albert.

They walk, a little more slowly than usual so that Albert can keep up, back to Violet's house. He tells them a story about how he and Eva once hung a rope swing from the oak tree for their son, Henry, when Henry was quite small, and how Henry did such amazing tricks on it

that the neighbors thought he was a monkey, which gives Violet and Rose the giggles.

Violet and Mama made a ginger cake not too long ago, and there is enough left for everyone to have a slice. When Rose's mama comes to collect her, she decides to stay for a piece too.

Vincent pours tea, Mama looks for a milk jug, and Violet gets some whipped cream out of the fridge in case anyone would like it with their cake.

When they are all busy chatting, Albert says quietly to Violet, "Is that another one of your small signs? I noticed it when you opened the fridge door."

He is pointing to the RIGHTS FOR HONEYMOONERS sign she made on the night of all the rain. So Violet explains about the shoestring book and the leaky washing machine and the Theory of Seeing Small Things.

"I see," says Albert.

Violet asks him to tell the story about the monkey swing again so Nicola and Dylan can hear it and she and Rose can giggle about it all over again. Then Rose's mama asks him about the hotel, and he tells them about the special herb garden he and Eva planted there and the French chef his son has recently found to cook lovely meals for the guests.

Much later on, Vincent says he will drive Albert home as it is far too late to walk.

"Before I go," Albert says to Mama and Vincent, "could I offer you both a couple of nights in the honeymoon suite at Chateau Trivelli to say thank you for everything you have done to save the oak tree? I don't suppose it will be much of a honeymoon really, though, since it's only down the road."

Violet and Rose both squeak with excitement, and Mama squeaks slightly too.

"It would be a *wonderful* honeymoon!" says Mama.

Vincent shakes Albert's hand and says thank you a lot of times, and Mama nearly shakes his hand but then gives him a hug instead.

A hotel with a beautiful garden

and a special French chef would be a perfect honeymoon for Mama and Vincent, Violet thinks.

Just before Vincent and Albert

leave, she whispers a small and secret suggestion into Albert's ear. She has taken the sign down from the fridge and points to the picture that she drew in the corner of a towel folded cleverly into the shape of a bird.

"I think that can be arranged," Albert whispers back.

The next weekend at Rose's house, when she and Violet have finished dinner and are in her bedroom making up a beautiful pink-and-white trundle bed for Violet to sleep in, the phone rings and it is Mama. She and Vincent are at Chateau Trivelli, and she wants to tell Violet all about the delicious five-course French dinner in the garden, and the spa, and most especially the towels that are folded like perfect birds. She has taken some photos of them to show Violet when she gets home.

In the background, Violet can hear Vincent excitedly saying, "Let me talk to her! Let me talk to her!"

"Vincent has some exciting news too," says Mama, laughing and saying good-bye.

"I just got a message from the *Clover Times*," says Vincent.

Violet beckons to Rose and holds

the phone between their ears so that she can listen to the message too. She suddenly has the feeling that the news will be important.

"Because of the protest, the council has agreed to build the parking lot somewhere else," says Vincent.

"They're *not* cutting down the oak tree?" checks Rose.

"They're *definitely* not cutting it down?" asks Violet, double-checking.

"Yes!" says Vincent. "You saved it!"

"One, two, two-and-a-half, three. Rose and Violet saved the tree!" chants Violet, bouncing up and down on the beautiful trundle bed.

"Three, four, four-and-a-half, five. Nests and acorns all survive!" chants Rose, scattering pink and white cushions all over her room.

They can hear Vincent and Mama laughing at the other end of the phone, and soon Rose's mama comes upstairs to see what all the excitement is.

Later, they all have hot chocolate with marshmallows to celebrate.

And when Vincent and Mama are back from their honeymoon and Violet, Rose, and Vincent start going to the park in the afternoons again, they sometimes go a bit later than they used to. Even though it is

a squish, they like sitting on Eva's bench with Albert, watching the oak tree's leaves go from gold to purple to navy blue and finally to black shadows against the darkening sky.

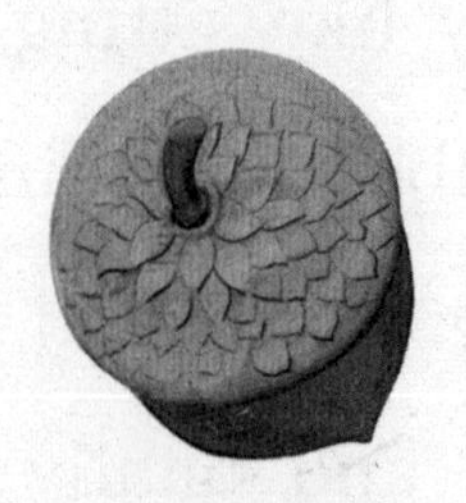